the

Didi Dodo FUTURE SPY

series

Book One: **Recipe for Disaster**
Book Two: **Robo-Dodo Rumble**
Book Three: **Double-O Dodo**

the

series

Book One: **Inspector Flytrap**
Book Two: **Inspector Flytrap in The President's Mane Is Missing**
Book Three: **Inspector Flytrap in The Goat Who Chewed Too Much**

By **TOM ANGLEBERGER**

with story consultant Oscar Angleberger

Illustrated by

JARED CHAPMAN

Amulet Books • New York

The Library of Congress has cataloged the hardcover edition as follows:
Names: Angleberger, Tom, author. | Angleberger, Oscar, consultant. |
Chapman, Jared, illustrator.
Title: Double-O Dodo / by Tom Angleberger ; with story consultant Oscar
 Angleberger ; illustrated by Jared Chapman.
Description: New York : Amulet Books, 2020. | Series: Didi Dodo, future spy ; book 3 | Summary:
When Didi Dodo and her friends hear that the queen was kidnapped by a human, they pose as a
family while searching for her at a new, human-themed amusement park.
Identifiers: LCCN 2019016536 | ISBN 9781419740978 (alk. paper)
Subjects: | CYAC: Kidnapping—Fiction. | Amusement parks—Fiction. | Spies—Fiction. |
Dodo—Fiction. Classification: LCC PZ7.A585 Dou 2020 | DDC [Fic]—dc23

Paperback ISBN 978-1-4197-4693-2

ABRAMS The Art of Books
195 Broadway, New York, NY 10007
abramsbooks.com

To the artist who gave Didi her famous sparkle: Jared Chapman!
—T. A.

CONTENTS

Opening . . . ix

PART 1
All's Fair in Love
and Rocket Pants . . . 1

PART 2
Undercover and
Overfed . . . 23

PART 3
Wiener Takes All . . . 53

GRAND FINALE
Until We Meat Again . . . 75

Epilogue . . . 94

Opening

My phone rang.

"Hello, this is Koko Dodo's Cookie Shop," I said. "Koko Dodo speaking! Would you like to hear about today's special cookie?"

"KOKO!" quacked the phone. "THIS IS THE QUEEN!"

The Queen is not really a queen. She is a duck who works with me in my cookie shop. She likes to wear a crown and call herself the Queen. That is OK with me, because she bakes really good cookies.

"Hello, Your Majesty," I said.

I'VE BEEN KIDNAPPED!

she quacked through the phone.

"What are you telling me about kidnapped?" I asked. "You're right here at the cookie shop baking today's special cookie."

"NO, I'M NOT!"

"Yes, you are."

"NO, I'M NOT!"

"Yes, you are."

"NO! I'M! NOT!"

"Yes, you are. I just saw you a minute ago."

"THAT WAS BEFORE I WAS KIDNAPPED!"

"Are you sure?"

"YES!"

The quacking was getting so loud I had to turn down the volume on my phone.

"LOOK AROUND THE SHOP, KOKO! I AM NOT THERE."

I looked around the shop.

There was a line of nine customers waiting to buy cookies. But there weren't nine cookies to sell them. In fact, there were no cookies. And there was no Queen!

I looked in the kitchen. There was a big pile of Royal Raisin Bars that didn't have raisins yet! And the Queen wasn't there to add the raisins!

"You're right," I said. "You're not here!"

"I KNOW THAT! I WAS JUST KID-NAPPED!"

"Who kidnapped you?"

"A HUMAN!"

"What are you telling me about a human?" I said. "Humans don't exist!"

"OH YEAH? THEN WHO KIDNAPPED ME?"

"That's what I was asking you," I said.

"OH, FORGET IT!" yelled the Queen, and then she hung up.

PART 1

All's Fair in Love and Rocket Pants

Chapter 1

Just then, Didi Dodo zoomed through the door on her roller skates.

She doesn't know how to stop, so she slammed right into the counter.

Usually when she does this, cookies fly everywhere, but not today.

"Hey, Koko, why didn't cookies fly everywhere when I slammed into the counter today?"

"Because the cookies aren't on the counter! Because the cookies aren't done! Because the Queen was kidnapped!"

"UH-OH!" squawked three of my customers, a cute little baby chick, another cute little baby chick, and a third cute little baby chick.

"Are there any clues?" asked Didi.

"Only one," I said. "The kidnapper was a human!"

"That's ridiculous!" said three of my customers, a unicorn, a dragon, and a tree that grows dollar bills. "Humans don't exist!"

"That's what I tried to tell the Queen," I said. "Oh, Didi, what are we going to do?"

"Why are you asking her?" asked the tree that grows dollar bills.

"She's Didi Dodo, Future Spy," I said. "She can do almost anything!"

"A future spy?" asked the unicorn. "Does that mean she comes from the future?"

"No," I said. "It means she is not officially a spy right now, but she will be someday, because she's always coming up with daring plans."

"Hmm," said the dragon. "How can you tell when she's got a daring plan?"

Didi Dodo waved one wing in the air!

Didi Dodo held her beak high!

Didi Dodo looked at us with sparkling eyes!

"I have a daring plan!" she announced. "We are going to skate around the city and . . . look for a human!"

"That doesn't sound very daring," said three of my customers, two bats and a horse who is the President of the United States.

"The daring part is that we're going to use my new, untested rocket pants!" shouted Didi.

"UH-OH," said all nine of my customers.

Chapter 2

What are you telling me about rocket pants?" I asked. "They sound TOO daring!"

"They are the fastest way for us to get around the city looking for a human," said Didi. "Let me slip into the restroom and put them on."

While she was in the restroom, one of my customers started to ring the little bell by the cash register.

"I want cookies and I want them now!" neighed President Horse G. Horse.

"I'm sorry," I said. "We don't have any cookies."

"Make some! NOW!" demanded the President.

"I'm sorry, I've got to go with Didi Dodo to find the Queen."

"NO! MAKE ME MY COOKIES! AND MAKE THEM THE BIGGEST COOKIES EVER!"

"No," I said. "I'm not going to make any cookies."

The President stamped his hooves.

"I'm going to call the FBI and have you arrested!" he yelled as he galloped out the door.

"I guess we'll come back later," said the dragon, the unicorn, the tree that grows dollar bills, and the two bats. "Good luck finding the Queen!"

Now the only customers left were the three cute baby chicks.

"I'm sorry, cute baby chicks," I said. "I don't think there will be any cookies today."

"We don't want cookies," said the first chick.

"We want to go with you and Didi," said the second chick.

"To save the Queen!" said the third chick.

"No, these rocket pants sound pretty dangerous," I said. "You'd better stay here."

"If we stay here, we'll poop on the chairs," said the cute baby chicks.

"OK, you can come," I said.

Just then, the restroom door blew open.

There were smoke and flames and a crazy *FWOOOOOSH* sound!

Suddenly, Didi Dodo blasted out of the restroom, grabbed me with one wing and the three baby chicks with the other, and then zoomed us all out the front door and into the street!

"UH-OHHHHHHHHHHHHH!" said the three baby chicks.

Chapter 3

Do you see a human?!" yelled Didi Dodo.

"No!" I yelled back. "Do you?"

"I have my eyes closed!" she yelled back.

"What are you telling me about closed eyes?" I screamed. "How can you steer with your eyes closed?"

"I can't steer with them closed!" she yelled back. "But I can't steer with them open, either. There's no way to steer rocket pants!"

"UH-OH," said the baby chicks.

"This plan was TOO DARING!" I yelled. "If you can't steer, we're going to run right into that statue!"

"What is it a statue of?"

"Johann Sebastian Bach," said the first baby chick.

"No, that's Wolfgang Amadeus Mozart," said the second baby chick.

"I'm pretty sure it's Pyotr Ilyich Tchaikovsky," said the third baby chick.

WHAM!

We smashed right into a statue of Ludwig van Beethoven.

But it wasn't a statue!

If it had been a statue, it would have been made out of rock or metal and would have hurt a lot worse.

This was kind of soft and smooshy.

"Hi, I'm Ludwig van Beethoven," said the not-a-statue.

"My daring plan worked!" shouted Didi, turning off her rocket pants. "We found a human!"

"If you're looking for a human, you came to the right place," said Ludwig van Beethoven. "Welcome to Humanland!"

"What are you telling me about Humanland?" I asked.

"I'm telling you that you have arrived at the World's Newest and Greatest Theme Park: Humanland," said Ludwig van Beethoven.

"What are you telling me about—" I started, but Didi interrupted me.

"I think I understand," she said. "This is a theme park and the theme is humans. So, all the rides, games, and mascots are human-themed."

I looked around and saw that she was right! It was like a huge fair. There were rides, games, gift shops, food stands, the world's biggest meatball, and blaring music. And, just like Didi had said, everything was themed after famous humans.

"This place is crazy!" I gasped.

"There's Inspector Flytrap and Nina riding on King Arthur's Merry-Go-Round-Table!" I said.

"Look! There's DJ Funkyfoot swinging through Tarzan's Bungee Jungle," Didi said.

"UH-OH!" hollered the baby chicks. "There's Cousin Yuk Yuk and Mimi Kiwi riding into Romeo and Juliet's Tunnel of Kissing! BLECH!"

Every ride was packed with plants and animals and had a big line of more plants and animals waiting to get on next. And every game, food stand, and gift shop was just as crowded.

There were twenty-three pig scientists standing in line just for a chance to sit down.

But mixed in with all these normal animals, there were lots and lots of humans: presidents, artists, athletes, movie stars, royalty, musicians, game show hosts, and every other type of human I had ever read about in a book or seen in a movie.

"Freaky," said the little baby chicks.

Suddenly, Ludwig van Beethoven took off his head. I am glad to be telling you that it wasn't a REAL head! It looked like it was made of foam or something. And Beethoven wasn't a REAL human. He was a wolf in a big, puffy mascot suit.

"OK, birds," said the wolf. "Tickets to Humanland cost $139.95 . . . each! Pay up!"

PART 2

Undercover and Overfed

Interlude

We paid for our tickets. It was a lot of money, but we had no choice if we wanted to find the Queen.

"My daring plan worked TOO well," said Didi. "We found lots of humans! Or, at least animals wearing big foam human heads. This MUST be what she meant. Somehow we have to find the one who kidnapped the Queen."

"Then let's get started!" I yelled, waving my wing, lifting my beak, and trying to make my eyes sparkle. "Now that we're in Humanland, nothing is going to stop me from finding the human who took her!"

"Nothing?" asked the three baby chicks.

"Nothing!" I said.

"What about a really mean yak?" asked the first baby chick.

"No way!" I said.

"What about a big sea monster?" asked the second baby chick.

"No way!" I said.

"What about an adorable little lost baby zebra?" asked the third baby chick.

"Huh?" I said. "If a mean yak and a sea monster couldn't stop me, how could a baby zebra?"

"Because it's really, really, really cute and adorable," said the third baby chick.

"And it looks like it lost its mommy," said the second baby chick.

"And it's right over there!" said the first baby chick.

"Uh-oh," I said.

Didi and I looked where the baby chicks were pointing. There was a baby zebra. It was really, really, really cute and adorable. And it looked like it had lost its mommy.

"I lost my mommy!" cried the baby zebra in a way that was really, really, really cute and adorable but also so sad that it stopped me and Didi in our tracks.

"I'd like to add something to my daring plan," said Didi.

"Do you mean helping the baby zebra look for its mommy while we look for the Queen?" I asked.

"Exactly!" said Didi.

"Fwank yoo," said the baby zebra. "Yoo nice."

And it held my wing with its tiny hoof.

Chapter 4

Psst," whispered Didi, barely shaking her wing, keeping her beak low, and definitely not eye-sparkling at all. "I have a plan."

"What are you telling me with just 'a plan'?" I asked. "Isn't it a daring plan?"

"No, it's a sneaky plan," said Didi. "We are going to pretend we're just a normal family here to enjoy a day at Humanland."

She took off her hat and sunglasses and put them in one pocket of her coat. Then she pulled two wigs from another pocket. She put one on and handed me the other.

"I'll be the mom and you be the dad," she said.

"What are you telling me about mom and dad?" I asked as I took off my hat and put on the wig.

"It's a disguise," said Didi. "We'll never find the Queen if we zoom around in rocket pants all day. We've got to sneak around. So we'll go undercover as parents with four adorable children."

"Who are the adorable children?" asked the three baby chicks and the baby zebra.

"You are, of course," said Didi.

"WE'RE HUNGWEE!" yelled the first baby chick.

"BUY US STUFF!" screamed the second baby chick.

"WE WANT FOOD ON A STICK!" shrieked the third baby chick.

"AN WE WUNT IT NOW!" hollered the baby zebra.

"Remember your manners, children," said Didi in a motherly voice. "How do you ask nicely?"

"PUH-LEEEEEZE," said the zebra and the chicks.

"Very good," she said in the same mom voice. "We'll all go get some corn dogs."

"YAY!"

"ME FIRST!"

"NO! ME FIRST!"

"WAHHH!"

Then in her regular voice, Didi whispered, "Keep your eyes peeled for the Queen, a kidnapper dressed in a human costume, and the baby zebra's mommy."

Chapter 5

O h my stars! Do you know how much corn dogs cost at the park? Nine dollars! And an extra dollar for the stick.

And there was a huge, long line. And the line was full of moms, dads, and kids, just like we were pretending to be.

"You were right, Didi," I said. "These are great disguises."

"Thanks," said Didi. "But my sneaky plan isn't working. We haven't found the Queen or the mommy. And it's impossible to tell who is in that Elvis costume."

Then she switched to her motherly voice again.

"Children, stop poking each other with your corn-dog sticks!"

"IT'S HOT AND WE'RE THIRSTY!" said the zebra and the chicks.

"OK, children," said Didi. "Let's go over there and get some drinks!"

She pointed at a booth that had a big sign that said:

RED GLOOP WITH
EXTRA SUGAR
$8

"YAY!"

"ME FIRST!"

"NO! ME FIRST!"

"WAHHH!"

"Do you want that in the special collector's cup?" asked the fox who was selling the red gloop.

"YES!" yelled the zebra and the chicks.

"And do you want extra extra sugar?"

"YES!" yelled the zebra and the chicks.

"How about extra red color?"

"YES!" yelled the zebra and the chicks.

"Great, that'll be fourteen dollars each!" said the fox.

The kids guzzled the red drinks. Didi and I looked around. No duck and no zebra. We did see a couple of Vikings, Queen Nefertiti, Scott Joplin, and Count Dracula, but we still could not tell what kinds of animals were inside the puffy costumes.

"NOW I HAF TO GO POTTY," said the baby zebra.

"OK," said Didi, "let's all go find a restroom."

"We don't have to go," said the baby chicks, "because we pooped on the chairs at the corn-dog place."

Chapter 6

After the baby zebra used the potty, we had a quick meeting.

"I haven't seen a single duck or zebra anywhere in this food court," whispered Didi. "So let's head to another part of the park."

"That is a good thing!" I whispered back. "Because we have spent all of our money!"

But when we got out of the food court, things got even worse. A huge sign said: NOW ENTERING PRICEYTOWN! Everybody was trying to sell us something!

"OK, children," said Didi in her motherly voice. "Be mindful that we won't be able to buy anything else. We're just looking."

We saw a stand called Now Ear This. A lion was selling hats with foam human ears.

"Can I get that?" asked the first baby chick.

"No, you'd only wear it once and then it would just take up space," said Didi.

"WAH!" cried the first baby chick.

Then we saw a cart where a cougar was using an airbrush to paint a picture of Leonardo da Vinci on a T-shirt.

"Can I get that?" asked the second baby chick.

"No, you already have one at home and you never wear it," said Didi.

"WAH!" cried the second baby chick.

Then we passed a tiger with a big bunch of balloons shaped like US presidents.

"Can I get an Eisenhower balloon?" asked the third baby chick.

"No, you'd let it go and then it would float away and you'd make a big fuss."

"Probably true," muttered the third baby chick.

Then we passed a gift shop where two bobcats were stacking drinking glasses that said "Humanland 1987!"

"Can I git zat?" asked the baby zebra.

"No, you'd only break it," said Didi.

"WAH!" cried the baby zebra.

Then we passed a place called Raul's Really Big Ramps. No one asked for a ramp.

Then I thought I saw the baby zebra's mom!

"Look," I said, "I think I see a zebra over by the carnival games!"

We ran over to the carnival games.

"My mistake," I said. "It wasn't a zebra. It was an okapi. Sorry."

Unfortunately, now the kids had seen the carnival games.

"Uh-oh," Didi and I said.

"I wanna play Stub-A-Toe!" said the first baby chick.

"I wanna play Catch-A-Kid!" said the second baby chick.

"I wanna play Pick-A-Nose!" said the third baby chick.

I waited to hear what the baby zebra wanted to play.

But it didn't say anything because it wasn't there!

"The lost baby zebra is lost again!" I shouted.

"Uh-oh," said the baby chicks.

"Let's retrace our steps," said Didi.

We ran back to PriceyTown.

"There he is!" shouted Didi. "At that glue booth!"

A huge grizzly bear was yelling at the little baby zebra.

"When I say come buy yourself some glue, I mean COME BUY YOURSELF SOME GLUE!"

"Uh huh," sniffed the little baby zebra.

"OK buddy? IS THAT CLEAR?"

"Uh huh."

"So you WILL come over here and you WILL buy some glue and you WILL enjoy it or you WILL HURT MY FEELINGS!"

"OK."

Just as we got there, the bear was handing the little baby zebra a tiny glue stick.

"Is this your kid?" growled the bear.

"No, I mean, yes," I said, remembering that I was pretending to be the zebra's dad.

"WELL THEN PAY UP!!!!!" roared the bear.

"What are you telling me with the pay up?" I said. "I don't have any money left. And anyway, we don't want your glue."

The grizzly bear roared and waved its huge claws.

"I WANT MY MONEY!" bellowed the bear. "AND ALSO A SINCERE APOLOGY! MY FEELINGS ARE VERY HURT!"

The bear jumped out of the glue booth and started to chase us!

"Run for your lives!" I screamed.

"The bear's too fast!" shouted Didi. "Everybody, jump on my back!"

We jumped on her back.

"Hold on tight!" she yelled and fired the rocket pants.

FWOOOOOSH!

First, we smashed into the lion selling hats. Foam ears went everywhere!

The lion roared, waved its huge claws, and started to chase us!

Then we splashed into the cougar painting T-shirts. Paint went everywhere!

The cougar roared, waved its huge claws, and started to chase us!

Then we crashed into the tiger selling balloons. Balloons went everywhere!

The tiger roared, waved its huge claws, and started to chase us!

Then we bashed into the two bobcats stacking glasses! Broken glass went everywhere!

The bobcats roared, waved their huge claws, and started to chase us!

"I hope you have a daring plan!" I yelled. "Because we're surrounded by large and very angry cats!"

"Yes," said Didi. "I do have a daring plan! Hold on tight! We're headed straight for Raul's Really Big Ramps!"

"Uh-oh," said the baby chicks.

We hit Raul's biggest ramp and went flying into the air.

We flew right out of PriceyTown, right over the Fun Fun Tube Slide, and ALMOST right into the giant meatball!

At the last second, Didi turned off the rocket pants and we dropped out of the sky and into a trash can filled with old corn dogs.

"This is all your fault!" the baby chicks yelled at the baby zebra.

"I dint do anyfing!" wailed the baby zebra.

"Children!" yelled Didi. "Do you want to spend the rest of the day in time-out?"

Everybody glared at everybody.

I groaned.

"We've made a huge mess! We've spent all our money! And we're all miserable and mad at each other!" I yelled. "This is terrible!"

"No, it's perfect!" said Didi. "Just like a real family!"

PART 3

Wiener Takes All

Interlude

Yep," said Didi Dodo. "Our undercover
operation is going so well, no one
here has any idea who we really are!"

"KOKO! DIDI!" someone yelled.

It was Penguini! We were standing right
in front of his food stand.

A big sign said: EAT PENGUINI'S SPUG-ETTI
CONES!

"Welcome my friends, KOKO and DIDI, to Penguini's Humanland Food Stand."

"Please, Penguini, don't say our names," whispered Didi. "We are undercover as a normal family. Pretend you do not know us."

"AH! I understand," said Penguini. "Then maybe you would like to eat some of my spug-etti cones? Normal families love them!"

"What are you telling me with the spug yeti?" I asked, looking around for Bigfoot.

"It's spaghetti in a cone so you can eat it while you walk around the park!" said Penguini.

"Genius!" said the first baby chick.

"Brilliant!" said the second baby chick.

"Delizioso!" said the third baby chick, who can speak Italian.

"WE WUNT IT NOW!" yelled the baby zebra.

"But I'm all out of money!" I yelled back.

"They are free for you, my friends who I pretend I do not know," said Penguini.

He served us six spug-etti cones. Each cone was filled with spaghetti, sauce, and meatballs.

"What do you say?" asked Didi in her motherly voice.

"Fank yoo," said all the baby animals.

"It IS delizioso!" I said. "Penguini, you are truly a master chef!"

"Thank you so much, dodo I pretend I don't know," said Penguini. "But if I was a true master, I could figure out how to make Spaghetti-on-a-Stick! That would sell even better than spaghetti in a cone! But . . . it is not so easy!"

Penguini took us into his food stand's kitchen, where there were boxes and boxes of corn dogs.

He picked up a corn dog and put spaghetti on it. The spaghetti slid off onto the floor.

"Have you tried wrapping the spaghetti around the corn dog?" asked Didi.

"Yes, but then the meatballs roll off," said Penguini, sadly. Then he got happy again. "By the way, have you seen my giant meatball?"

Penguini waved a flipper at the giant ball of meat that loomed over his food stand.

"Amazing!" said Didi. "What keeps it from rolling away?"

"It's propped up by a bronze statue of the famous Greek warrior Achilles."

"Hmm," I said. "To me that doesn't seem like a very safe way to prop up a giant meatball!"

Chapter 7

Just then, Galileo walked up to Penguini's food stand.

Of course, it was not really Galileo; it was another mascot. He took off his big foam head.

Underneath was a puffin.

"Hey, Penguini!" said the puffin.

"Hey, Puffini!" said Penguini. "Are you ready for lunch?"

"No, thanks," said the puffin. "I had a corn dog already. But now I want some dessert!"

"Have a cannoli, my friend," said Penguini.

He handed the puffin a cannoli, which is sort of like a cookie with extra cream.

The puffin ate it, said thank you, then put its big foam human head back on and walked away.

"I just came up with a new plan!" said Didi. I was glad she was talking in her normal voice again.

"Is it a daring plan?" I asked.

"No," said Didi, "it's a yummy plan!"

"How can a yummy plan help us find the Queen?" I asked.

"By helping us find the kidnapper!" said Didi.

"Huh? How?" asked the baby chicks.

"When the Queen said she was kidnapped by a human, we thought she meant a real human," said Didi.

"But humans aren't real!" said the first baby chick. "These mascots are all animals in human costumes!"

"Right," said Didi. "And now we know the kidnapper is just using one of the costumes as a disguise."

"But which one?" asked the second baby chick. "There are so many mascots!"

"Right," said Didi. "So we need to get all the mascots to take their big foam heads off."

"But the kidnapper won't do that!" insisted the third chick. "If they are hiding inside a mascot suit, they will want to stay hidden. They can't risk being filmed by a security camera or seen by someone who knows them."

"Right!" said Didi. "So if all the normal mascots take off their heads, then the only mascot with a head would be the kidnapper!"

"That's a really smart plan," chirped the baby chicks.

"It is," I said. "But how will you get them to take off their big foam heads?"

"I won't," said Didi. "YOU WILL!"

"What are you telling me about me?" I asked.

"Koko, you need to create a cookie so yummy that all the mascots will want to take off their heads to eat it!"

"Then we grab whichever human is left and make it free the Queen!" cheered the baby chicks.

"It sounds yummy AND daring," I said.

"Can yoo do it?" asked the baby zebra.

"Of course, I can do it," I said, waving my wing, lifting my beak, and putting my baker's hat back on. "I'm Koko Dodo!"

Chapter 8

Penguini offered to let me use his kitchen and any of the ingredients he had.

"Anything to help save the Queen!" said Penguini.

"Anything?" I asked.

"Anything!"

"OK," I said. "Everyone be quiet for a moment so I can imagine the perfect cookie."

Everyone was really quiet, but outside I could still hear the screams from the roller coaster and the whines from the teenagers and the music from loudspeakers on every light pole.

And then all of those sounds faded away and I had a vision.

It was a vision of the perfect cookie for the job.

It was a vision of a corn dog that was more than a corn dog, a cookie that was more than a cookie, and a stick that was more than a . . . well, OK, the stick was still just a stick.

It was a vision of . . .

"THE COOKIE DOG!" I shouted.

"What are you telling us about a cookie dog?" asked everybody.

"I am telling you about the greatest thing to happen to fair food since the funnel cake," I replied. "Now, everybody, please wash your wings, hooves, and/or flippers! I'll need your help!"

While I used the cannoli ingredients to make cookie dough, the others unboxed the corn dogs.

Then we rolled the corn dogs in the dough and started baking them. Then we dipped them in my supersweet icing and covered them with sprinkles.

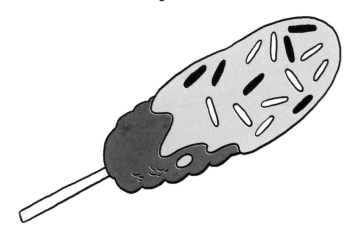

They smelled yummy.

"Those smell yummy," said Genghis Khan, who happened to be walking by.

"Have one for free," I said.

"Thanks!" said Genghis Khan. "First let me take off this big foam head."

Underneath the big foam head was a cheetah. He took a big bite out of the cookie dog. "It tastes as good as it smells!"

"It works," said Didi Dodo. "But the smell won't reach all the way across the park. We need some other way to let all the mascots know about the free cookie dogs."

"I'm the official park announcer," said the cheetah. "I'll head back to my office and make the announcement right now!"

And he ran off really fast!

"Wow, that was lucky," said the baby chicks.

Mini Cookie Dog Recipe!

To make a true Cookie Dog, you need to have all of
Penguini's kitchen stuff. But you can easily make
one of these Mini Cookie Dogs in your own kitchen.

YOU WILL NEED:

- 1/2 cup of confectioners sugar (Don't use regular
  sugar! You'll just end up with a wet hot dog!)
- 1 can Vienna sausages
- 1 quart-sized Ziploc bag about half full of cereal
  (Try different cereals for different tastes!)
- A bowl
- Measuring spoons
- Straws

DIRECTIONS:

1. Don't open the can of sausages yet! Settle down!
   And don't take the cereal out of the bag yet
   either! Sheesh!

2. Use the can like a rolling pin to crush the cereal
   in the bag. Keep rolling the can back and forth
   until the cereal is a fine powder.

3. Put the confectioners sugar into the bowl.

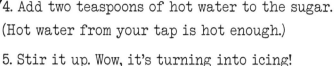

4. Add two teaspoons of hot water to the sugar. (Hot water from your tap is hot enough.)

5. Stir it up. Wow, it's turning into icing!

6. Add another teaspoon of hot water and keep stirring. Is it good and runny yet? If not, add another teaspoon of water.

7. Once the icing is good and runny, open the can of sausages. Put one sausage into the bowl and roll it around in the icing.

8. Insert a straw into the sausage. It's just like a corn dog on a stick, except the straw is a lot safer!

9. Holding the straw, insert the sausage into the bag of cereal powder. Shake.

10. Remove the sausage from the bag, and you've got a Mini Cookie Dog! ENJOY!!!!

GRAND FINALE
·······················
Until We
Meat Again

Chapter 9

ATTENTION, MASCOTS! ATTENTION, MASCOTS! FREE COOKIE-DOGS-ON-A-STICK RIGHT NOW FOR ALL MASCOTS! HEAD TO THE GIANT MEATBALL FOR YOUR FREE COOKIE DOGS! DON'T WAIT! ACT NOW! SUPPLIES ARE LIMITED! VOID WHERE PROHIBITED!"

Mascots started showing up immediately.

"Can I get a free Cookie-Dog-on-a-Stick?" asked a caveman.

"Me too?" asked Alexander Hamilton.

As Penguini and the others started giving away cookie dogs, Didi and I hopped on the Ferris wheel so we could get a good look at what happened next.

"I do not like high places!" I moaned. "I am a cookie baker! I just want to be in my kitchen!"

"Settle down," said Didi. "If you want to save the Queen, you need to open your eyes and help me look around."

I looked around. Every mascot in the park had stopped posing for pictures and was running to get their free cookie dog! It was like a stampede!

And then, as soon as each one was served, they took their big foam head off to eat!

From up on the Ferris wheel, we could see it all!

"There's the wolf who sold us our tickets!"

"There's Puffini the puffin! I guess he was still hungry."

"There's an elephant! How did it even fit that trunk inside the foam head?"

"LOOK!" shouted Didi. "There's Queen Nefertiti!"

"What are you telling me about Queen Nefertiti?" I asked. "Isn't she a human?"

"Yes!" said Didi. "But she hasn't taken off her head yet!"

"She isn't even getting a Cookie-Dog-on-a-Stick!" I said. "Isn't she hungry?"

"She's looking around suspiciously!" said Didi. "I think she's figured out what's going on!"

"She's making a run for it!" I cried.

"Let's catch her!" yelled Didi.

"But how can we catch her?" I groaned. "We're stuck at the top of the Ferris wheel!"

"This is the daring part of the plan,"
said Didi, with a wave, nod, and sparkle.

Then she grabbed me by the wing and
jumped off the Ferris wheel!

"NOOoooooooooo!" I cried as we fell.
"It's too daringgggggg . . ."

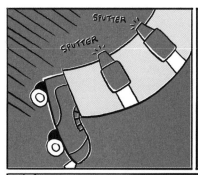

Chapter 10

Queen Nefertiti's headed for the waterslide!" I shouted. "Do you think we can catch her?"

"I've got a better idea," said Didi. "Let me borrow your phone."

I gave her my phone and she called Inspector Flytrap.

"Hey, Flytrap! Ask your goat to bite a leg off the statue of Achilles that is propping up the giant meatball."

"Funny you should ask," said Flytrap. "She's already chewing on it right now!"

"Big heel," said Nina.

She bit right through Achilles's leg. The statue snapped in two, and the meatball started rolling.

"Gotta go!" yelled Flytrap, and he hung up.

Seconds later, he and Nina went zooming past us on their skateboard.

"That's the fastest meatball I've ever seen!" yelled Inspector Flytrap. "Run for your lives!"

He was right. The giant meatball was thundering straight at us!

"It's going to crush us!" I shouted.

"Hold on!" yelled Didi.

She fired her rocket pants, and we shot into the air just a second before the meatball rolled under us.

By the time we landed, it had already rolled onto the waterslide. That's when it really started going fast!

"The kidnapper is about to get clobbered!" said Didi with a smile. "All we have to do now is watch."

The mascot and the meatball whooshed around curves, through dips and loops, toward the huge, scary, steep drop at the end.

Queen Nefertiti was fast, but the meatball was faster!

"It's gaining on her," said Didi, with an even bigger smile. "There's no escape!"

Just then we heard a loud QUACK!

"That was the Queen's quack!" I said. "Not the human queen, the DUCK QUEEN!"

"QUAAAAAACK!"

"Actually, I think it's both!" shouted Didi.

"What are you telling me?"

"I can't explain it," said Didi. "But the quacking is coming from Queen Nefertiti! The Queen is the queen!"

"And she's about to be squashed by a giant meatball!" I yelled.

"Not if me and my rocket pants can help it!" shouted Didi. "I have a brand-new daring pla—"

The rocket pants started beeping and a tiny little "low fuel" light started blinking.

"Oh no!"

"Oh no!"

QUAAAAAAAAAAAACK!

The queen and the meatball had just gone over the edge of the huge, scary, steep drop!

"Please, please, please tell me that you have a brand-new brand-new daring plan!" I said.

"I do," said Didi. "Wait here. I've got to do this myself."

She skated full speed toward Tarzan's Bungee Jungle and grabbed a vine.

"HEY! I WUZ NECKST IN LINE!" yelled an angry yak, but it was too late, Didi was already swinging toward the waterslide.

In that last split second before the meatball smashed into the ground with a disgusting meaty crash, Didi swung through the air and grabbed the queen.

And in that very very last split split second, the bungee vine yanked them both back to where I was standing.

They were both covered in spaghetti sauce and waterslide water, but they were safe!

The cute baby chicks rode up on the baby zebra just in time to see Queen Nefertiti take her big mascot head off.

It really was the Queen inside.

"Quack," she said.

"WHAT IS GOING ON?" asked EVERY-BODY except the baby zebra.

"I can answer that," said the baby zebra.

"How can YOU answer that?" asked EVERYBODY except the baby zebra.

"Because I'm not really an adorable, lost baby zebra," said the baby zebra.

"What are you telling us?" asked EVERYBODY except the baby zebra.

"I'm not even a baby zebra," said the baby zebra. "I'm actually Double-O Debra, head of the Secret Spy Agency."

"I've never heard of you or that agency," I said.

"That's because we're a secret agency and we're really good at keeping secrets," said Debra.

"Hmm," said the baby chicks.

"I can promise you that the spy agency is as real as I am," said the Queen.

"Real?" I asked. "Do you mean that you're really . . ."

"Yes," said the Queen. "I really am the Queen."

"She really is," said Double-O Debra. The tiny zebra pushed a button on her watch and a huge limousine rolled up. The doors opened and lots of guards, knights, royal advisors, and trumpet players jumped out. They all made a big fuss over the Queen.

"ALL HAIL THE QUEEN OF WING-LAND!"

"Wingland?" I gasped. "I didn't even know she was Winglish!"

No one answered me because they were all bowing to each other and yelling "hur-rah" and throwing rose petals. Then they all got back in the limo and drove away . . . with the Queen!

"What just happened?" I yelled. "Why did the Queen kidnap herself and make Didi come up with all those daring plans all day and make me make all those cookie dogs and make the baby chicks . . ."

"I said I could answer that, and I will," said the baby zebra, I mean, Double-O Debra. "It was a test."

"What are you telling me about a test?" I yelled.

"We had to be sure that Didi was ready," said Double-O Debra.

"Ready for what?"

"Ready to become a Secret Spy, of course," said Double-O Debra. "And she is!"

Double-O Debra handed Didi a badge.

"Welcome to the Secret Spy Agency, Double-O Dodo," she said.

Epilogue

I was very happy when Didi got her badge. But the next morning, when I unlocked my cookie shop and started baking cookies, I wasn't happy.

I was lonely.

Without Didi and the Queen, baking cookies was going to be dull and boring.

I'd be stuck in my kitchen, while the Queen was having royal balls at the palace and Didi was out having daring plans to save the world.

Even sprinkling sprinkles on a batch of frosted sugar cookies didn't make me feel better.

And then some of my tears fell into my brownie batter and I had to throw it out.

Just then, the door burst open!

Didi zoomed in on her roller skates and smashed right into the sugar cookies. Frosting and sprinkles went everywhere!

"What are you telling me?"

"I'm just making sure it's safe for the Queen to come in and get to work," said Didi, looking behind the counter and under the sink.

She pressed a button on her watch.

A huge limo pulled up outside.

The Queen hopped out and waddled in the door.

"What are you doing here, Your Majesty?" I asked.

"I'm here to work," she quacked.

"What are you telling me about work?" I said. "You're the Queen!"

"Yes," she said. "And that means I can do anything I want. And I want to make cookies!"

"Actually," I said, "today we're baking a cake."

"What are you telling us about a cake?" asked Didi and the Queen.

"We thought you only baked cakes on special occasions," said the three baby chicks, walking in the door.

"This is a VERY special occasion!" I shouted, waving my wing and all that. "So it will be a VERY special cake!"

"Yum! What kind?" asked Double-O Debra, who had been hiding behind a big can of frosting.

"It'll be a fish-flavored, corn-dog cookie cake with secret fudge sauce letters that say: Didi Dodo, Secret Spy!"

"That's a very daring cake," said Didi. "Do you dare to make it?"

"I do," I said. "Do you?"

We did! And everyone baked happily ever after!

ABOUT THE
AUTHOR AND ILLUSTRATOR

TOM ANGLEBERGER is the *New York Times* bestselling author of the Origami Yoda series, as well as many other books for kids. He created Koko Dodo with his wife, Cece Bell, for the Inspector Flytrap series. When that series ended, he still wanted to send Koko on some bigger adventures . . . whether Koko wanted to go or not! Visit Tom at origamiyoda.com.

JARED CHAPMAN is the author-illustrator of the best-selling *Vegetables in Underwear*, as well as *Fruits in Suits* and *Pirate, Viking & Scientist*. He lives in Texas. Find out more about Jared at jaredchapman.com.

Crack open another case in

DJ Funkyfoot: Butler for Hire!

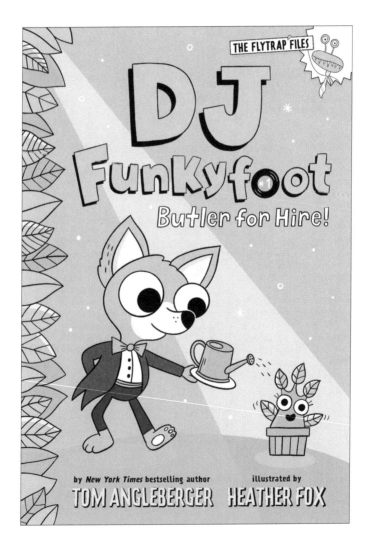

Opening

My phone rang.

"Greetings," I said. "I am DJ Funkyfoot, and I am at YOUR service."

"Good," said a prickly voice. "I'm Cactus Kwame of Cactus Kwame's Roller Rink and Disco Rodeo. I need a DJ for our big Disco Rodeo Roller Boogie Contest tonight!"

"Ah," I said. "I'm afraid you have made a common mistake, sir."

"No way!" said Cactus Kwame, and he was extra prickly. "I never make a mistake."

"Yes, sir," I replied, even though I knew he HAD made a mistake. I am a butler who serves tea, not a DJ who plays music.

"So can you come over and play us some crazy disco beats tonight or not?"

"I'm afraid not, sir," I said. "As I was trying to tell you: I am not a DJ."

"Whoa! Hold up! Aren't you DJ Funkyfoot?"

"Yes, sir."

"But you're telling me you're not a DJ?"

"No, sir," I said.

"Then why do you call yourself DJ Funkyfoot?!" yelled Cactus Kwame.

I did not yell back. I remained calm. I have had a lot of training to become a

butler, and part of that training is not getting mad.

"My parents named me DJ Funkyfoot because they hoped that I would someday become a hip-hop star."

"Well?" asked Cactus Kwame. "Did you become a hip-hop star or not?"

"No, sir," I said, "I became a butler."

"A butler?"

"Yes, sir."

"What does a butler do?"

"I do whatever my employer needs me to do," I said. "For example, I might prepare a cup of tea in the early evening."

"I don't want a cup of tea in the early evening!" yelled Cactus Kwame. "I want crazy disco beats all night long!"

"I don't do that."

"But it'll be on TV! I thought you hip-hop stars loved to be on TV!"

"I'M NOT A HIP-HOP STAR! I'M A BUTLER!"

"Well, you must not be a very good one if you go around yelling at people like that!"

He was right! I had forgotten my training! I wasn't being a good butler!

"I am so sorry, sir," I said, but Cactus Kwame had hung up.

PART 1

Butler
for Hire!

Chapter 1

My phone rang.

"Greetings," I said, reminding myself to be polite no matter what the other person said. "I am DJ Funkyfoot, and I am at YOUR service."

"Great!" said a stressed-out voice. "We want to hire you!"

"Very good, ma'am," I said. "But before you hire me, I must make sure you know that I am not a hip-hop star."

"Why would I want to hire a hip-hop star?" asked the stressed-out voice.

"I don't know, ma'am," I said, "but many people do and—"

The stressed-out voice interrupted me.

"I don't need to hire a hip-hop star. I need to hire a nanny!"

"I'm sorry, ma'am, but I am not a nanny either."

"What are you?"

"A butler, ma'am."

"That's close enough!" yelled the stressed-out voice. "We can't afford to be picky. Another nanny just quit on us! That makes forty-three! And you're the only nanny I can find."

I had to remember my politeness training.

"Again, ma'am, I am a butler, not a nanny."

"Who cares? It's the same thing!"

"Excuse me, ma'am, but a nanny and a butler are not the same thing. In fact, there are some very important differences to—"

The stressed-out voice interrupted me again.

"I don't have time to quibble!" yelled the stressed-out voice. "Get over to Murky Pond Park right now!"

The stressed-out voice hung up.

The adventure continues in

DJ Funkyfoot #1:
Butler for Hire!